BILLY

Based on *The Railway Series* by the Rev. W. Awdry

Illustrations by

Robin Davies and Jerry Smith

EGMONT

4
2
7
6
1

3
5
Annie

EGMONT
We bring stories to life

First published in Great Britain 2008
by Egmont UK Limited
239 Kensington High Street, London W8 6SA

Thomas the Tank Engine & Friends™

CREATED BY BRITT ALLCROFT

ISBN 978 1 4052 3785 7
1 3 5 7 9 10 8 6 4 2
Printed in Italy

The Forest Stewardship Council (FSC) is an international, non-governmental organisation dedicated to promoting responsible management of the world's forests. FSC operates a system of forest certification and product labelling that allows consumers to identify wood and wood-based products from well-managed forests.

For more information about Egmont's paper-buying policy please visit www.egmont.co.uk/ethicalpublishing

For more information about the FSC please visit their website at www.fsc.org

TO THE TRAINS →

This is a story about Billy, a shiny orange engine. When Billy arrived at my railway, I asked Thomas to show him what to do. Billy thought that Thomas was bossy, but he soon realised that Thomas was just being helpful …

One morning, Thomas the Tank Engine was at Brendam Docks. He was excited.

"Today I am going to look after a new engine," peeped Thomas to Salty.

The new engine arrived. He had an orange coat and was puffing with pride. "I'm Billy," he whistled. "Let's go!"

"Wait, Billy," peeped Thomas. "We can't go yet. We have to wait for The Fat Controller. He will tell us what to do."

BILLY

The Fat Controller soon came to meet Billy.

"Billy," he boomed. "You have a very busy day. First, you must take empty chicken vans to the farm and bring the chickens back to the Docks. Then you are to deliver diesel fuel to the Quarry. And lastly, you have to take coal to the Depot."

"Yes, Sir!" bubbled Billy, happily.

"Thomas, you must show Billy how to be a Really Useful Engine," added The Fat Controller before he left.

BILLY
1
2991

"Billy," Thomas steamed. "You must pull the chickens slowly and smoothly."

"I know that," sighed Billy. He pumped his pistons impatiently.

"Don't pump your pistons before you are ready to leave," whistled Thomas. "It wastes coal and water. Now, first you must take on more coal and water for your busy day," he added.

"Thomas!" huffed Billy. "Stop telling me what to do. You are a very bossy engine!"

BILLY

Billy raced off without Thomas.

"He thinks you're a bossy boiler, me hearty!" laughed Salty.

Thomas didn't like being called bossy. But he had promised The Fat Controller he would look after Billy.

So, Thomas chased after him.

BILLY

Thomas was pleased to find Billy at the farm, but Billy wasn't pleased to see Thomas.

"Billy! You must take on coal and water," he said.

"Don't tell me what to do, Thomas!" huffed Billy. "You are a very bossy engine!" And he steamed off to the Quarry.

"Silly Billy, you've forgotten the chickens," Farmer McColl called out.

"Bother him!" wheeshed Thomas. And he chuffed quickly off after the impatient engine.

BILLY

Thomas was pleased to find Billy at the Quarry, but Billy wasn't pleased to see him.

"You didn't pick up the chickens!" puffed Thomas. "And you still haven't taken on more coal and water!"

"Stop telling me what to do, Thomas!" huffed Billy. "You are a very bossy engine!"

Billy steamed off.

Mavis gasped, "He's forgotten our diesel!"

Thomas was worried. He raced after Billy.

BILLY

Thomas was pleased to find Billy at the Depot, but Billy wasn't pleased to see him.

Billy had backed up to heavy trucks of diesel oil.

"They need this diesel oil at the Quarry *now*!" peeped Thomas. "And you *still* haven't taken on coal and water!"

"Stop telling me what to do, Thomas!" huffed Billy. "You are a very, very bossy engine!"

Billy steamed off without the diesel oil.

Thomas was very worried. He chased after Billy.

1
BILLY
DIESEL

Thomas was pleased to find Billy at the Coaling Plant.

Billy was backing his trucks under the hopper, but he didn't see Percy there, and he biffed him … right under the hopper!

Percy was covered in coal, from funnel to footplate!

"Watch out, Silly Billy!" Percy peeped.

"Oh, no!" puffed Thomas. "You must be careful when you roll under the hopper. And you *must* take on coal and water *now*!"

"Thomas!" huffed Billy. "Stop telling me what to do! You are a very bossy engine!"

Thomas was very unhappy. He didn't want to be called bossy any more. "Do whatever you want, Billy!" he wheeshed.

This made Billy very happy, and he raced off. But suddenly, Billy came to a stop. He had run out of coal and water!

BILLY

"Cinders and ashes!" cried Thomas, when he saw what had happened. "I haven't taught Billy to be Really Useful at all!"

Thomas shunted Billy to the Water Tower. Billy's firebox was filled with coal while he took on water.

"I know you think I'm a bossy boiler," puffed Thomas, "but I've done all these jobs before. I can help you. Then no one will call you a Silly Billy!"

BILLY

Together, Billy and Thomas collected Farmer McColl's chickens and took them to the Docks. Then they delivered the diesel oil to Mavis and Diesel at the Quarry. And lastly they delivered the coal to the Depot.

Now Thomas and Billy were very tired.

BILLY

"Goodbye, Billy," Thomas chuffed. "The Fat Controller will be very pleased that you finished all your jobs."

Thomas started to puff away.

"Thomas!" bubbled Billy. "You're not a bossy boiler. You're a Really Useful Engine. And I really enjoyed working with you."

Thomas felt very happy. Billy wasn't a Silly Billy any more. And Thomas had made a really good friend!

BILLY

3
5
Annie

The Thomas Story Library is THE definitive collection of stories about Thomas and ALL his friends.

5 more Thomas Story Library titles will be chuffing into your local bookshop in 2009!

Stanley

Flora

Colin

Hank

Madge

And there are even more Thomas Story Library books to follow late

So go on, add to your Thomas Story Library NOW!

A Fantastic Offer for Thomas the Tank Engine Fans!

STICK POUND COIN HERE

In every Thomas Story Library book like this one, you will find a special token. Collect 6 Thomas tokens and we will send you a brilliant Thomas poster, and a double-sided bedroom door hanger! Simply tape a £1 coin in the space above, and fill out the form overleaf.

TO BE COMPLETED BY AN ADULT

To apply for this great offer, ask an adult to complete the coupon below and send it with a pound coin and 6 tokens, to:
THOMAS OFFERS, PO BOX 715, HORSHAM RH12 5WG

☐ Please send a Thomas poster and door hanger. I enclose 6 tokens plus a £1 coin. (Price includes P&P)

Fan's name..

Address..

....Postcode................................

Date of birth...

Name of parent/guardian..

Signature of parent/guardian..

Please allow 28 days for delivery. Offer is only available while stocks last. We reserve the right to change the terms of this offer at any time and we offer a 14 day money back guarantee. This does not affect your statutory rights.

☐ Data Protection Act: If you do not wish to receive other similar offers from us or companies we recommend, please tick this box. Offers apply to UK only.